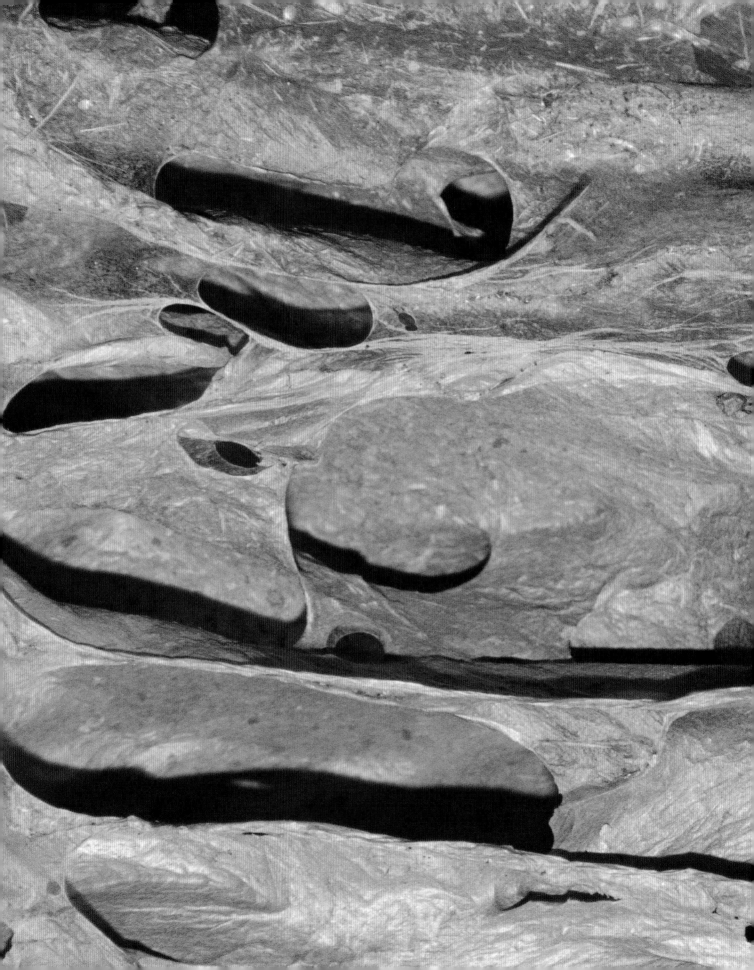

ANTS

by Liza Jacobs

BLACKBIRCH®
PRESS

San Diego • Detroit • New York • San Francisco • Cleveland • New Haven, Conn. • Waterville, Maine • London • Munich

For more information, contact
The Gale Group, Inc.
27500 Drake Rd.
Farmington Hills, MI 48331-3535
Or you can visit our Internet site at http://www.gale.com

No. 274-1, Sec.1 Ho-Ping E. Rd., Taipei, Taiwan, R.O.C.
Tel: 886-2-2363-3486 Fax: 886-2-2363-6081

LIBRARY OF CONGRESS CATALOGING-IN-PUBLICATION DATA

Jacobs, Liza.
  Ants / by Liza Jacobs.
     v. cm. — (Wild wild world)
  Includes bibliographical references and index.
  Contents: About ants — Amazing strength — Many kinds of food —
Termites and ants.
   ISBN 1-4103-0054-4
   1. Ants—Juvenile literature. [1. Ants.] I. Title. II. Series.

QL568.F7J33 2003
595.79′6—dc21   2003001424

Table of Contents

About Ants

Ants are everywhere!
There are more than
10,000 different kinds of
ants in the world. They live
all over the earth, except
in cold polar areas. Ants
are insects. They are very
social and live in groups
called colonies. All the
members of a colony work
together to find food, care
for the young, build the
nests, and protect each
other. There are usually
more females than males
in a colony.

Amazing Strength

Ants have amazing strength! They carry things much larger and heavier than they are. Ants have inner and outer jaws. The outer jaws are called mandibles. They use them to pick up things. An ant's mandibles are very sharp and are also used for biting, cutting, and digging. Even with all this strength, ants can use their mandibles gently, too.

Sensing the World

Ants have two long antennae on their heads. The antennae are an ant's main way of sensing the world around it. They wave them around and tap them on things to pick up signals of movement or smell. Antennae help an ant "talk" to other ants, find food, and sense its way around. Ants often clean their antennae with their front legs to keep them in tip-top shape.

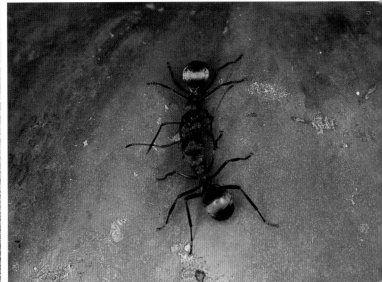

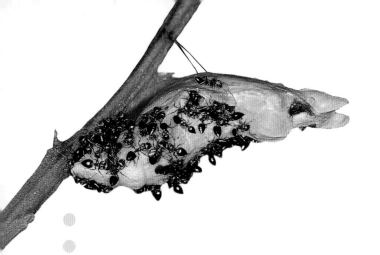

Many Kinds of Food

Ants eat many kinds of food. They drink juices from plants and "milk" certain kinds of insects for their liquid. They also eat caterpillars, worms, beetles, bees, termites, and many other kinds of insects.

Some ants eat leaves, fungus, fruit, seeds, or honey. They like foods that are sweet and will eat many types of human food.

In a colony, different kinds of ants have special jobs. Worker ants are female. They often work together to capture a large meal and carry it back to the nest.

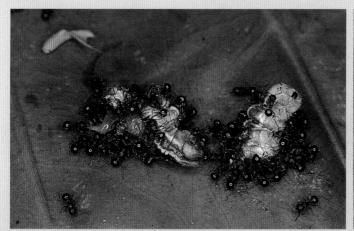
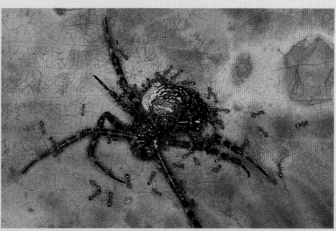

11

Queens and Workers

Like many other insects, ants go through four stages of life as they grow into their adult forms. The four stages are egg, larva, pupa, and adult.

Each colony has one or more queen ants. Queens are the biggest ants in the colony. It is their job to mate and lay eggs. Many queens have wings until they lay their eggs. Then their wings come off.

Worker ants bring the queen food. Special worker ants called nurse ants also help her take care of the young and the nest.

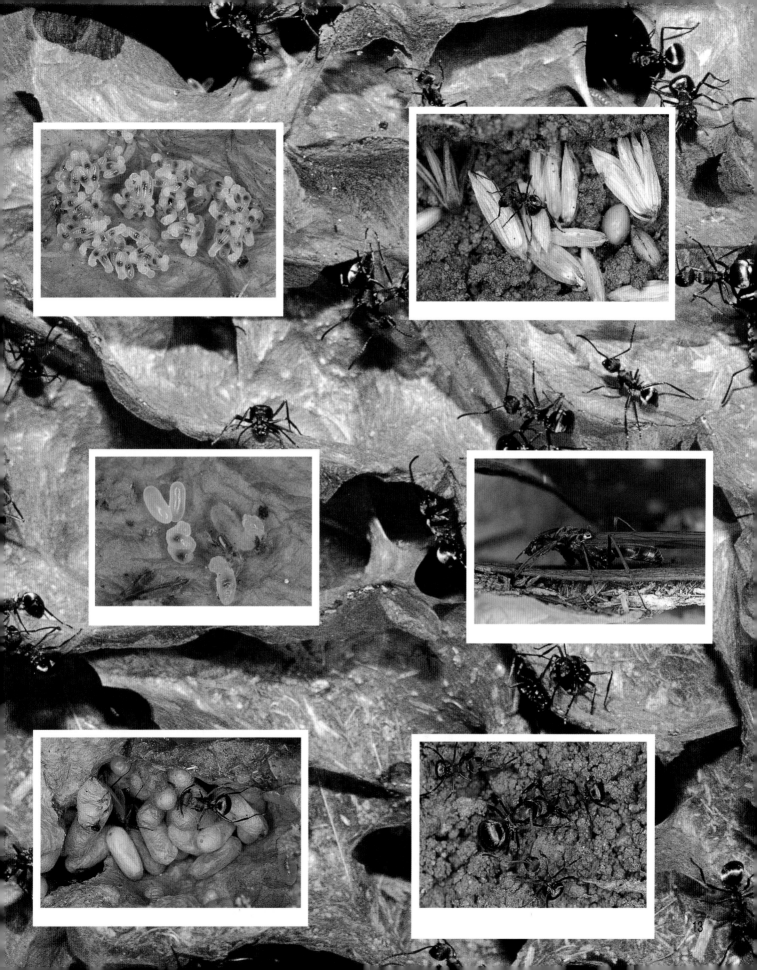

Larvae

A queen licks her eggs to keep them clean. In about 20 days, they hatch and enter the second stage of ant life. This is the larva stage.

Ant larvae look like small white worms. They do not have any legs and cannot see. While the workers help the queen, soldier ants protect the nest.

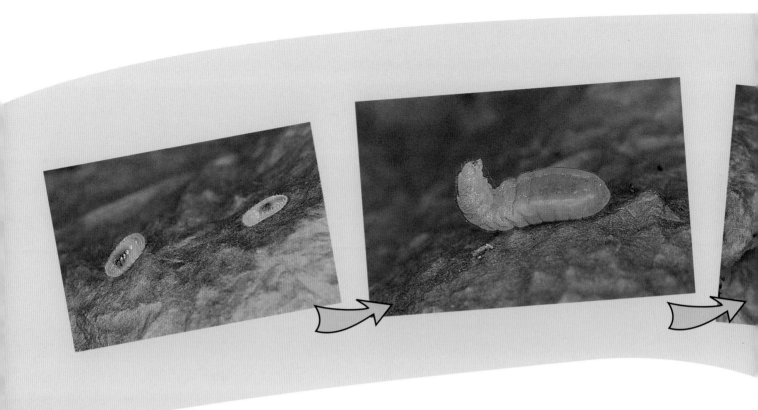

Pupae

Ant larvae cannot take care of themselves. The queen and nurse ants continue to care for and feed them. After about a month, the larvae are ready to enter the third stage. This is the pupa stage.

Some ants spin a cocoon around their bodies. Others do not. During the pupa stage, the adult body forms. It takes about 3 weeks for the adult ant to fully form. Then it comes out of its cocoon. At first, the adults are pale. But their color darkens quickly.

Mating

When the new adults come out of the nest, it is time for them to mate. The male ant's main job is to mate with the queen.

During this early adult stage, many kinds of ants have wings. After mating, males usually die. Females lose their wings. Other females that have mated become queens.

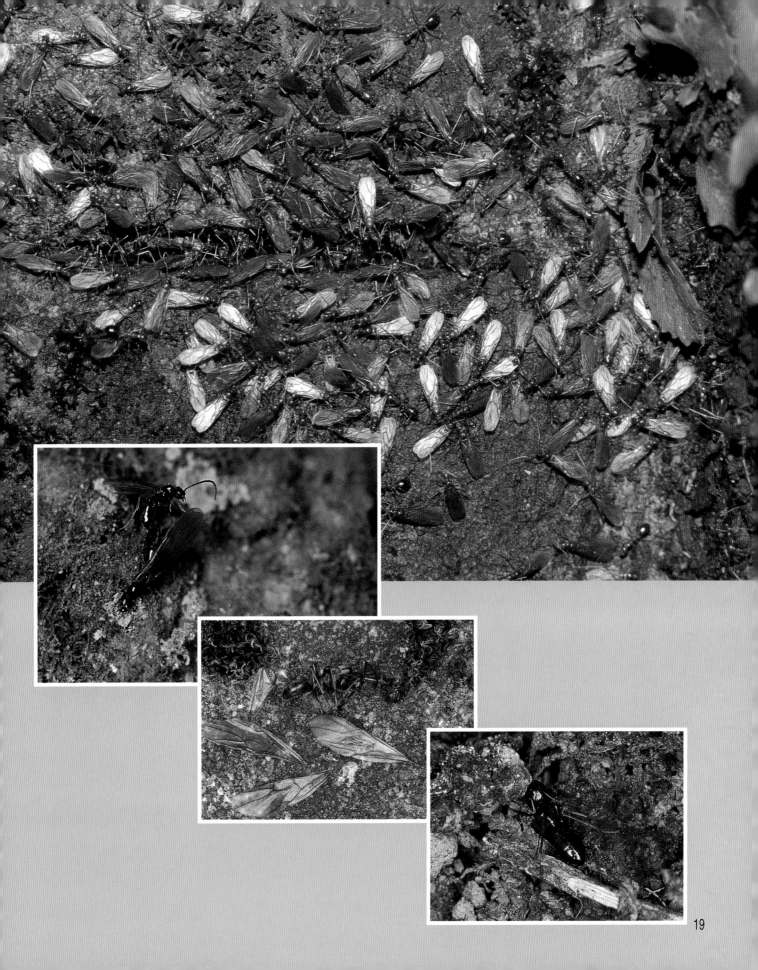

19

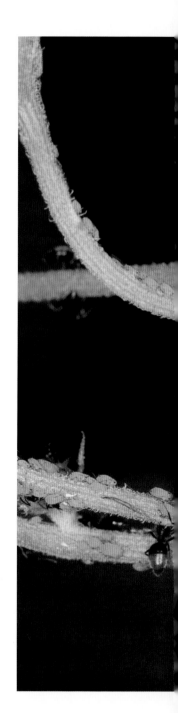

"Milking Aphids"

One incredible thing about ants is that they "farm" certain kinds of insects for food. They do this in much the same way that farmers take care of cows for their milk.

Small, green insects called aphids make a sweet liquid called honeydew. Ants actually herd rows of aphids and collect this honeydew by tapping them with their antennae. They bring the liquid back to the nest to share with their fellow ants. In exchange, ants protect aphids from insects that would eat them. Ants do this with a few other types of insects, too.

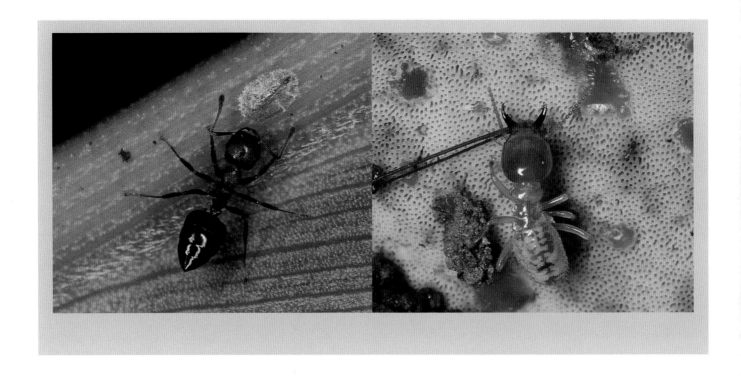

Termites and Ants

Some kinds of ants are often confused with termites. All of the insects shown here, except for the top left picture of an ant, are termites.

Termites are closely related to ants. They both live in colonies that work together and are led by a queen. But there are important differences. Termites eat wood, while carpenter ants only chew holes in wood. You can easily tell them apart, too. Ants have a tiny waistline in front of their abdomens and termites do not. And while an ant's antennae have an "elbow" that bends, termites have straight antennae.

For More Information

Pascoe, Elaine. *Ants (Nature Close-Up)*. San Diego, CA: Blackbirch Press, 1999.

Stefoff, Rebecca. *Ant.* New York: Marshall Cavendish, 1998.

Glossary

colony a group of ants

larva the second stage of an ant's life

mandibles an ant's outer jaws

pupa the third stage of an ant's life

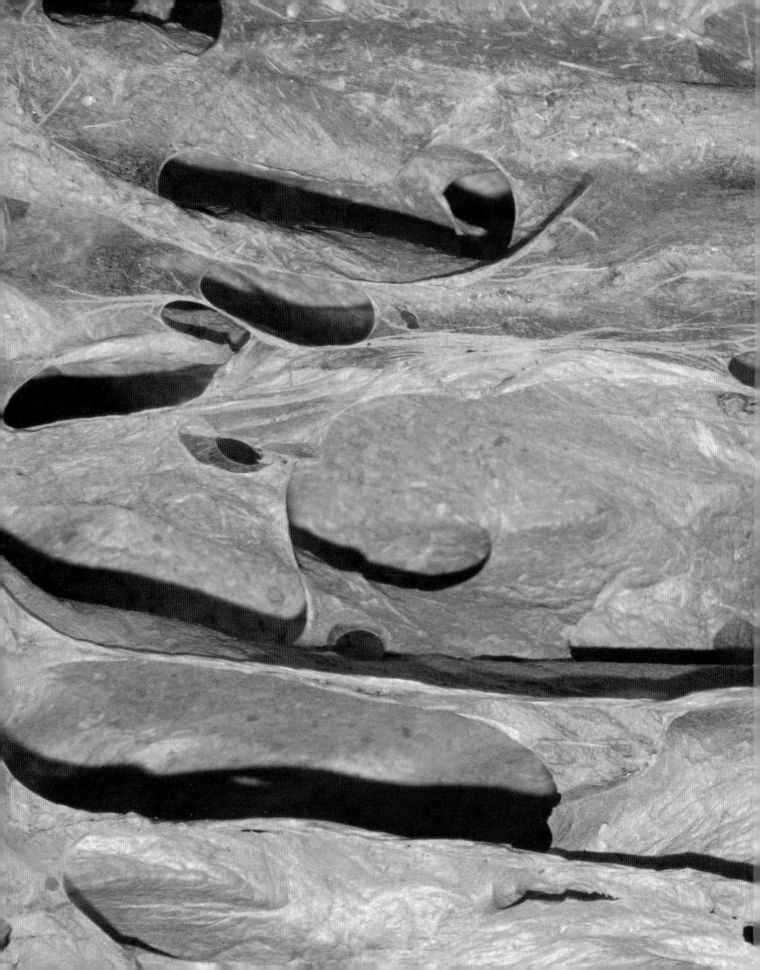